Spring Bee

GROSSET & DUNLAP
Penguin Young Readers Group
An Imprint of Penguin Random House LLC

© The Hive Enterprises Ltd. All rights reserved. Published in 2016 by Grosset & Dunlap,
an imprint of Penguin Random House LLC, 345 Hudson Street, New York, New York 10014.
GROSSET & DUNLAP is a trademark of Penguin Random House LLC. Manufactured in China.

ISBN 978-1-101-99500-6   10 9 8 7 6 5 4 3 2 1

It was a sunny day in the meadow, and Buzzbee and Jasper were practicing their soccer skills.

"Wait until you see my new trick!" Jasper told Buzzbee.

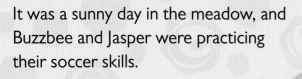

Jasper bounced the ball on his head three times.

Then he sent the ball flying across the meadow.

"Wow! Cool!" Buzzbee said to Jasper.

The ball landed on the far side of the meadow with a *thud*. It rolled to a stop beside a single flower.

"Where did that silly plant come from?" Jasper asked.

"I don't know," Buzzbee said. "It wasn't here yesterday."

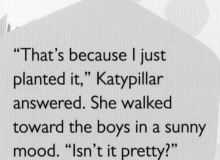

"That's because I just planted it," Katypillar answered. She walked toward the boys in a sunny mood. "Isn't it pretty?"

Jasper didn't agree. "I don't want that plant here. This is our soccer field," he said.

"We always play here," Buzzbee explained to Katypillar. "It's the best place to play."

"Yes," Katypillar agreed. "That's why the queen chose it for the party."

"PARTY?" Jasper and Buzzbee shouted in surprise.

"It's a 'hello to spring' party!" Katypillar explained. "Tomorrow we're going to celebrate the start of spring. That's why this lovely plant is here."

Katypillar's plant had a big pink flower growing on the top. She seemed very proud of it.

"But what about our soccer field?" Jasper asked.

"Sorry, boys. I'm afraid you'll have to find somewhere else to play." Katypillar waved and left the meadow.

Jasper let out a sigh.

"Silly flower," he said. He kicked the ball toward the plant.

Buzzbee caught the ball in time. "Careful, Jasper!" he said. "Let's move and play somewhere else."

But Jasper was annoyed. "If anyone should move, it's the silly plant!"

He grabbed the ball from Buzzbee and bumped into the flower.

A single petal fell to the ground.

"Oh no!" Buzzbee gasped.

"Don't worry." Jasper giggled. "There's plenty more petals."

Jasper walked up to the flower and gave it a good shake.

"See? It's fine."

"Jasper!" Buzzbee said. "Katypillar planted it especially for the party. She's going to be upset. We have to make it better."

"Okay," Jasper agreed. "But what can we do?"

"We've got to try to put the petals back on."

Buzzbee grabbed a single petal and placed it back on the plant. The petal fell to the ground. He picked it up and tried again. But the petal fell to the ground again.

"It's not working!" Buzzbee cried. "What else can we try?"

Jasper thought hard. "Can't we just get some petals from somewhere else?"

"That's a brilliant idea!" Buzzbee agreed. He knew just how to solve their problem.

Buzzbee flew to the hive, where Rubee was doing crafts.

"Can I borrow this?" Buzzbee asked. He needed pink paper. "And these?" He grabbed the scissors and tape.

"Okay," Rubee agreed curiously.

Buzzbee thanked her and left with the supplies. He had to work on his plan to save Katypillar's flower.

Back in the meadow, Buzzbee cut out paper petal shapes. Then he taped the paper petals to the stem of the plant.

"Wow! That's brilliant," Jasper said.

But Buzzbee wasn't sure.

"I don't know, Jasper. I don't think it looks like it did before. I think I'd better fetch Katypillar."

Jasper looked at Buzzbee and sighed. "I'll go. I was mean to the plant."

The boys brought Katypillar back to the meadow to show her Buzzbee's paper petals. She didn't look too happy.

"Sorry, Katypillar," Buzzbee said. "We didn't mean to hurt it."

"Sorry," Jasper added.

Buzzbee pulled off his paper petals. His plan had not worked very well.

"That's all right, boys." Katypillar sighed. "I don't think it was your ball. The flower is just a bit unhappy in its new home."

"Unhappy?" Buzzbee asked. "We could cheer it up! Banana sandwiches make me feel better."

Jasper joined in. "And pollen stoppers make me happy!"

Katypillar shook her head. "Unfortunately, I don't think those will work for this poor little plant."

Buzzbee had an idea!
"What about a song?
That always works
when Babee is sad."

"Hmm . . . That's not a bad idea,"
Katypillar said. "I do know a
springtime song . . . Here goes!"

Spring
is sprung,
Spring is sprung,
all the leaves come out today,
Blossom blooms and floats away,
Birds will sing, and bees will play,
Spring is sprung.

Spring is Sprung

Spring is Sprung,
all the leaves come
out today,
Blossom blooms
and floats away,
Birds will sing,
and bees will
play,
Spring is
Sprung.

"All together now!" Katypillar said to the boys. They joined in the song and danced.

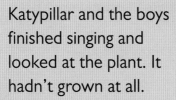

Katypillar and the boys
finished singing and
looked at the plant. It
hadn't grown at all.

"Oh dear," Katypillar
said. "It won't be much
of a spring party without
a flower."

Buzzbee agreed.
"It looks really sad."

"There's no more we can do today,"
Katypillar told the boys. "We'll
just have to wait and see how it is
tomorrow." She said good-bye
and left the meadow.
The boys could tell she
was worried.

Buzzbee leaned close to the
flower and whispered, "Bye,
flower. Please get better for the
party. Everyone is coming to
see you."

He flew back to the hive with
Jasper for the night. They both
hoped the flower would grow.

The next day, the meadow was abuzz! All of the hive's residents gathered around the plant to wait for the queen.

"Oh dear," Grandma Bee said when she saw the little plant.

"My poor flower!" Katypillar cried. "And the queen is due any minute!"

Jasper looked at the plant sadly. "I don't think the queen is going to like this very much."

Honk! Honk!

The queen had arrived! Lord Bartlebee announced Her Majesty to the crowd. As the queen said hello, Buzzbee and Jasper looked at the plant. A new flower was starting to bloom!

Buzzbee tried to get Katypillar's attention, but she told him to be quiet.

"*Shh*, Buzzbee, the queen is here!"

The flower was growing faster!

"Look! Look!" Buzzbee whispered again.

"Oh yes," the queen told the crowd. "Do look, everyone. How lovely!"

WOW!

A beautiful pink flower had bloomed behind the crowd!

"Spring has sprung!" Buzzbee shouted.

The crowd *ooh*ed and *aah*ed at the flower.

"Well done," Buzzbee told the flower. "I'm very pleased to see you!"

Jasper leaned in close to talk to Buzzbee.

"I've thought of another place to play soccer, Buzzbee. So the flower will be safe!"